DOLPHINS IN DANGER

Dear Riley,

My friend, Dr. Poole, an expert on dolphins and whales, has invited us to the South Pacific island of Moorea to study spinner dolphin behavior and communication.

Do you know how spinners get their name? Dr. Poole will explain that and a whole lot more! Aunt Martha, Cousin Alice, and I can't wait to go. See you soon in a dolphin lagoon!

Uncle Max

ADVENTURES OF RILEY

BY AMANDA LUMRY
& LAURA HURWITZ

EaglemonT
Press

ILLUSTRATED BY
SARAH McINTYRE

A special thanks to all the scientists who collaborated on this project. Your time and assistance was very much appreciated.

All photographs by Amanda Lumry except:
pgs. 10-11 humpback whale © Mike Hutchings/Reuters/CORBIS
pgs. 14-15 spinner dolphin © Jay Syverson/CORBIS
pg. 29 spinner dolphin © Amos Nachoum/CORBIS

Illustrations ©2005 by Sarah McIntyre
Editing and Finished Layouts by Michael E. Penman

Digital Imaging by Embassy Graphics, Canada
Printed in China by Midas Printing International Limited
ISBN: 0-9748411-1-0

A portion of the proceeds from your purchase of this licensed product supports the stated educational mission of the Smithsonian Institution - "the increase and diffusion of knowledge." The name of the Smithsonian Institution and the sunburst logo are registered trademarks of the Smithsonian Institution and are registered in the U.S. Patent and Trademark Office.
www.si.edu

2% of the proceeds from this book will be donated to the Wildlife Conservation Society.
http://wcs.org

A royalty of approximately 1% of the estimated retail price of this book will be received by World Wildlife Fund (WWF). The Panda Device and WWF are registered trademarks. All rights reserved by World Wildlife Fund, Inc.
www.worldwildlife.org

First edition published 2005 by
Eaglemont Press
PMB 741
15600 NE 8th #B-1
Bellevue, WA 98008
1-877-590-9744
info@eaglemontpress.com
www.eaglemontpress.com

Library of Congress Cataloging-in-Publication Data

Lumry, Amanda.
  Dolphins in danger / by Amanda Lumry & Laura Hurwitz ; illustrated by Sarah McIntyre.– 1st ed.
      p. cm. – (Adventures of Riley)
  Summary: Riley helps save a pod of dolphins that become trapped in a lagoon in Tahiti.
    ISBN 0-9748411-1-0 (hardcover : alk. paper)
  [1. Animal rescue–Fiction. 2. Spinner dolphin–Fiction. 3. Dolphins–Fiction. 4. Marine animals–Fiction.
5. Scientists–Fiction. 6. Tahiti–Fiction.] I. Hurwitz, Laura. II. McIntyre, Sarah, ill. III. Title.
  PZ7.L9787155Do 2005
  [Fic]–dc22
                                                    2004019519

Tweet! Tweeeet!

"For my trip, I need to practice surfing and talking to dolphins," said Riley.

"Dolphins won't understand you," said Riley's friend Mike. "Sure they will," said Riley. "People use whistles to teach dolphins tricks, don't they? I'm going to use my whistle to train the dolphins in Moorea."

When they landed on Moorea, it was midday and very hot.

"*Ia Orana* (Ya-or-ah-nah)! That's Tahitian for hello," Dr. Michael Poole greeted them.

"When can we see the dolphins?" asked Alice.

"If we hurry, we can spot them swimming in the lagoon right now," said Dr. Poole.

"Then I can teach them to do some tricks for us," Riley whispered to Alice.

Arrivée

2

➤ This ocean holds half of the Earth's unfrozen water.
➤ It is the largest and deepest ocean.
➤ Pacific means "peaceful".

Pacific Ocean

Dr. Paul Boyle, Director, New York Aquarium, Wildlife Conservation Society

"I can't wait to see the show!" said Alice as everyone climbed into the boat.
"What show?" asked Aunt Martha.

4

"The dolphin show," said Riley. "You know, where they do tricks."
"This isn't a theme park, Riley," said Uncle Max, "these are
wild dolphins in their natural environment."

5

Spinner Dolphin

➤ A dolphin travels in small groups (2 - 40 dolphins) called pods or larger groups of up to several hundred members called schools or herds.

➤ A dolphin is a mammal, not a fish, and must breathe air to survive.

➤ It can swim up to 25 mph (40km/h)!

Lisette Wilson, South Pacific Regional Marine Coordinator, World Wildlife Fund

SPLASH!

"Wow!" said Riley. Another dolphin twirled in the air. Riley and Alice clapped.

"How did you teach them to do that, Dr. Poole?" asked Alice.

"I bet you used a whistle!" added Riley.

Laughing, Dr. Poole said, "Spinning is how spinner dolphins get their name! They spin to remove remoras, which are fish that attach themselves to the dolphin's skin. They also jump as part of a play time, like school recess. It is my job to study and learn from the dolphins, not to teach them anything. Hmm...I don't know how the dolphins got in here. The nearest opening to the sea is very shallow and narrow, and I've never seen them use it before."

6

"That dolphin is missing part of its dorsal fin," noticed Uncle Max.

"That's Shark Bite," said Dr. Poole. "It was in a fight with a shark. To keep track of the dolphins, I give them names that I won't forget."

At dinner, they met Dr. Poole's sons, Temoana (Tay-mo-ah-nah) and Tearenui (Tay-ah-ray-noo-ee), and his wife, Mareva (Mah-ray-vah). The boys promised to take Riley and Alice surfing the next morning.

Breadfruit

➤ Breadfruit is usually oblong and large, weighing ten pounds (4.5kg) or more when ripe.

➤ Breadfruit is a member of the fig family.

➤ When roasted, breadfruit looks like freshly baked bread.

Dr. Warren Wagner,
Botany Curator,
Smithsonian
Institution

"Surf's up!" yelled Alice, as she zoomed by Riley.

"It sure looks easier on television," said Riley, as he wiped out again.

"Alice! You're a natural!" said Temoana.

A natural show-off, thought Riley.

"Look!" said Tearenui. "Humpback whales! They always return this time of year to have their babies. Let's go tell Papa."

"That whale is bigger than our boat," said Alice. "I hope it doesn't tip us over!"

"Accidents can happen if people approach whales too quickly or get too close, but if we respect them and give them some space, there is really very little danger," said Dr. Poole.

"I read that humpbacks can sing," said Riley.

"True," said Aunt Martha. "The songs they use to communicate are beautiful."

"When they sing, they point their heads straight down towards the ocean floor," added Dr. Poole.

"Cool!" said Riley and Alice.

"Hey, did you know that I can speak dolphin?" said Riley. He blew his whistle–*loudly*.

"OW! My ears!" said Alice.

Humpback Whale

➤ A whale's flippers are one-third the length of its body.

➤ It migrates between 2,000 - 3,000 miles (3,200 - 4,800 km) per year between colder waters and warmer waters.

➤ A baby humpback, called a calf, can weigh up to 3,000 pounds (1,360kg).

Dr. Howard Rosenbaum,
Director,
Cetacean Conservation Program,
Wildlife Conservation Society

"I think the dolphins would agree with you, Alice!" said Dr. Poole. "A plastic whistle just makes a loud noise that doesn't mean anything to them. Dolphins use special sounds when interacting with each other and to measure the size and location of an object. They may also communicate by the way they twirl and spin."

11

After watching the giant whales breach and blow, everyone cooled off in the lagoon and explored the world below.

Manta Ray
➤ It can weigh over 6,600 pounds (3,000 kg) and have a wingspan over 26 ft (8m)!
➤ During mating season, a ray will jump fully out of the water.
➤ It eats plankton, small shrimp or fish.

Paul Sieswerda, Aquarium Curator, New York Aquarium, Wildlife Conservation Society

Parrot Fish
➤ Its top and bottom front teeth grow together to form a beak.
➤ It uses its beak to bite off pieces of coral and eat the plants growing on them.

Dr. Victor G. Springer, Senior Scientist, Division of Fishes, Smithsonian Institution

➤ There are over 200 species of moray eels and scientists are still discovering new ones.
➤ An eel can grow over 6 ft (1.8m) long and may weigh over 100 pounds (45kg).
➤ It doesn't usually bite humans, unless it is surprised or bothered.

Dr. David G. Smith, **Moray** Eel
Museum Specialist, National Museum of Natural History, Smithsonian Institution

► A grouper is born as a female, but turns into a male after a few years.
► Lunging out from its coral hiding place, with a snap of its jaws it catches its prey in less than a second.

Dr. Carole Baldwin,
Research Zoologist,
Smithsonian Institution

Grouper

"Look!" cried Aunt Martha. "Spinner dolphins!"
"That's odd," said Dr. Poole, shaking his head. "They should have gone into the open ocean to feed last night and then returned to another part of the lagoon today. Something is definitely wrong."

14

Dr. Poole scratched his head. "We'd better get back to the lab. I should check my photos to see if these are the same dolphins we saw yesterday. They may be trapped in the lagoon and could starve. The food they need to survive can only be found out in the ocean."

15

As Uncle Max and Dr. Poole hurried off, the others stayed behind with Mareva. "I perform Tahitian dances every Friday night for tourists," she told them. "Would you like to watch me practice?" "Sure!" Alice nodded excitedly. "I take dance lessons back home."

Vanilla

➤ The vanilla plant is actually an orchid. Vanilla comes from a long bean-like fruit produced on its vines.

➤ The small black spots you see in some kinds of vanilla ice cream are the tiny seeds from inside the orchid bean.

John Kress, Research Scientist and Curator, Department of Botany, Smithsonian Institution

There she goes showing off again, thought Riley. "I think I'll go and see what Uncle Max and Dr. Poole are doing."

17

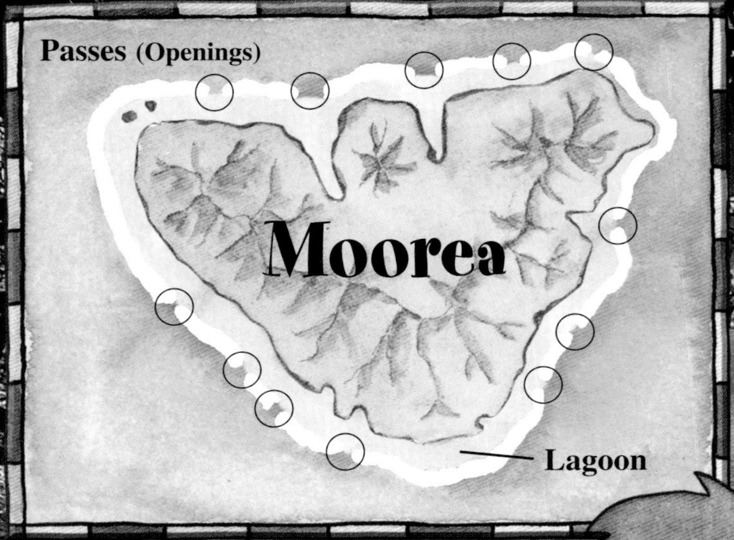

On his way to the lab, Riley saw Temoana's surfboard. *If I practice, I know I can be as good as Alice. Maybe I can talk to the dolphins while I'm at it.* Riley walked along the beach until he saw some small waves out past the lagoon.

Passes (Openings)

Moorea

Lagoon

Volcanoes and Lagoons

➤ Over time, some volcanoes sink into the ocean, and as they do, coral grows around them near the surface of the water. When the volcano sinks completely, it leaves a coral ring. The water inside this ring is a lagoon.

"Uncle" Maxwell Plimpton,
Professor,
Senior Field Biologist

He steered through the opening into the breaking waves.

19

20

Riley crashed headfirst into the water. Gasping, he panicked! Which way was up? Was it his imagination, or did he see a dark shape coming towards him ?

A gentle nudge pushed him to the surface. Brrrp! Blah! Salt water gushed out of his mouth. Suddenly, he felt himself being pulled from the water.

22

"Thank heavens we saw the missing surfboard and found you!" cried Aunt Martha.

"The surf out here by the coral reef is very dangerous!" said Dr. Poole.

"I know that *now*," said a red-faced Riley, rubbing his head. "But how did I get back to the surfboard?"

"Let me guess, you were saved by the dolphins," laughed Alice.

"No, really," said Riley. "I think I was."

"These are the same dolphins from yesterday. They look very tired and hungry," Dr. Poole said.

"I could blow my whistle!" said Riley. "If we make enough noise, they might be happy to leave."

"Good idea," said Dr. Poole. "But we may need some help in case they swim the wrong way."

"What about a hukilau?" asked Aunt Martha.

"A what?" asked Alice.

"A hukilau works like a net, but is only a rope with palm leaves hanging from it, so there is no danger of a dolphin's fins getting caught," said Aunt Martha. "I saw one in Hawaii."

Dr. Poole called for help.

Soon the lagoon was full of boats! They formed
two lines. The first line was full of dancers with metal
pipes and paddles to bang underwater and behind
them were fishermen with a long hukilau net.

27

"Riley, now's your chance!
Blow your whistle to start
our dolphin parade!"
said Dr. Poole.

Tweeet!

Tweet! Clang! Bang!

Clang!

Splash! Splash! Bang!

At first nothing happened. Then,
slowly, one dolphin swam forward, then
another, and another. Soon the dolphins
were at the opening. In a flash,
they were gone, returning
to the open sea.

28

"Look!" cried Riley.
Shark Bite leapt up right in front of him,
spinning in the air. Everyone cheered.
The dolphins were saved!

Spinner Dolphin

➤ A dolphin can dive 1,000 ft (300m) deep—that's like diving off a 100 story building!

➤ 6 - 8 million dolphins have been caught and killed in the Eastern Pacific Ocean since 1970 as a result of purse seine net fishing.

➤ It can spin up to 7 times in a single jump!

Dr. Michael Poole, Director, Marine Mammal Research Program, CRIOBE

29

That night, they watched Mareva perform.
"You are such a good dancer!" said Riley.
"Thank you," Mareva said. "And you are
an excellent scientist. You knew just how to save
those dolphins. We all have talents, but sometimes we
don't know it until the right moment comes along."
Riley blushed.

Black Pearl

➤ A pearl is usually the same
color as the mollusk that
produced it.
➤ Pearls come in all shapes
and sizes. Round ones are rare.
➤ An adult pearl oyster can pump
over 5 gal. (19L) of
water through its gills
every hour.

Mona Matepi,
Project Officer,
World Wildlife
Fund, Cook Islands

"Nets and loud noises can be used to trap and kill dolphins," said Dr. Poole. "Today we used these things to save their lives. By continuing to study how dolphins behave and communicate, we may find even more ways to work together to help them."

"And perhaps they can teach us a thing or two," said Aunt Martha.

31

Back home, Riley entertained everyone with his amazing dolphin rescue story. At the beach, he showed his family his new surfing skills. His father took pictures, which Riley sent to Alice. He returned to living the life of a nine year old, until he once again heard from Uncle Max. **Where will Riley go next?**

32

FURTHER INFORMATION

French Polynesia

Bora Bora
Huahine
Tahaa
Moorea · Papeete · Tahiti
Raiatea

Pacific Ocean

N · W · E · S

Dr. Michael Poole is a real scientist! An American marine biologist, he came to Moorea in 1987. In real life he is married to Mareva, who really is a Tahitian dancer, and they do have two sons, Temoana and Tearenui.

Dr. Poole is known around the world for his work with spinner dolphins and humpback whales. He helped create one of the largest marine dolphin and whale sanctuaries in the world to protect the marine life mammals in French Polynesian waters and beyond.

Glossary

BREACH: To leap out of the water and land back with a splash.

COMMUNICATE: To give information or messages by talking or moving.

CORAL REEF: A grouping of coral that forms a home for fish.

DORSAL: On or near the back.

ENVIRONMENT: The space where an animal lives, sleeps and eats.

GUSH: To pour or flow quickly and all at once.

HEMISPHERE: The north or south half of the Earth, separated by the equator.

LAGOON: An area of water separated from the sea or ocean, often by a coral reef or piece of land.

MIGRATE: To travel from one place to another, usually during a change of seasons.

MUCUS: Slimy stuff, such as the goo that comes out of your nose.

NUDGE: To push gently.

PANIC: To show sudden fear.

PURSE SEINE FISHING: A method used to catch tuna, using a net that is a mile long and several hundred feet deep. The net closes like a drawstring purse around the tuna and anything else in the area. The fishermen are supposed to give dolphins a chance to escape, but a mistake in a single fishing haul can mean the death or injury of 500 to 2,000 dolphins.

STARVE: To become weak due to lack of food.

Coral

Careful! Coral is alive and part of the reef. Touching or stepping on it can damage or even kill it. Without coral, fish have no reason to stay, and we would have nothing left to see.

WHAT IS THIS?

N · W — 1 — E · S

➤ Hidden inside each *Adventures of Riley* book is at least one hidden compass.
➤ Each one will unlock an on-line Further Adventure movie on Riley's website.

Visit Riley's World today!

www.adventuresofriley.com

Surfing Lesson: Riding waves while lying on a wooden board started in the Polynesian Islands over three thousand years ago. The first surfers were fisherman using "*paipo*" (known today as body boards) to ride waves back to shore, along with any fish they caught. Over time, riding waves became a pastime and not just a part of the fisherman's job.

CeleBRate!
in
CeNTRal AMERICA

BY JOE VIESTI AND DIANE HALL
PHOTOGRAPHED BY JOE VIESTI

LOTHROP, LEE & SHEPARD BOOKS • MORROW
NEW YORK

CENTRAL AMERICA

CARIBBEAN SEA

Ambergris Caye
San Pedro

BELIZE

GUATEMALA

Chichicastenango

HONDURAS

Santiago de
Sacatepéquez

Copán Ruinas

EL SALVADOR

Nahuizalco Sonsonate

NICARAGUA

Masaya

PACIFIC OCEAN

COSTA RICA

Puerto Limón

PANAMA

Las Tablas

Just as people do in the United States, people in Central America come together to celebrate holidays with song and dance, food and fun, parades and prayer. But the holidays and the ways in which they are celebrated often seem very different from our own. Almost everyone in Central America is Catholic, and most holidays have religious significance, even if they are secular celebrations as well. Almost everyone in Central America is also *mestizo*—a person of mixed Spanish and Indian ancestry. Throughout Central America individual communities have integrated Spanish and Indian traditions in different ways to create their own unique fiestas. But whatever and whenever the celebration, it is always a time to forget about workaday routines and to appreciate the really important things in life: family, beliefs, and traditions. What better way to meet the people of the world than at a celebration!

A shy angel graces a flower-covered float in the Holy Week procession in Nahuizalco, El Salvador.

GUATEMALA

EL DÍA DE LOS MUERTOS

(THE DAY OF THE DEAD)

Many Catholics believe that on November 1, All Saints' Day, the spirits of the dead revisit their earthly homes. Throughout Latin America the holiday is known as *El día de los muertos,* the Day of the Dead. Every year on this day, families gather to tend their relatives' graves and make offerings of food and flowers to welcome them home. Properly honoring the dead is believed to ward off illness, bad luck, and failed crops for the rest of the year.

In Santiago de Sacatepéquez, Guatemala (Santiago for short), people get up at sunrise on November 1 to decorate every door and window of their homes with bright orange marigolds and to prepare offerings of food and drink for their ancestors. Then they head for the hillside cemetery to decorate the graves of their loved ones. Later in the day, as the wind picks up, huge tissue-paper kites fill the skies over the cemetery. Each kite is ten to twenty feet in diameter and requires four or five strong young men to control it. (The young men take the opportunity to impress the young women of the village with their skill and strength.) The kites are flown all afternoon, until the wind dies down at sunset. They will brighten the sky again on November 2, All Souls' Day. Later, they will be burned to honor the spirits of the dead.

A family mausoleum is decorated with a fresh coat of paint and wreaths of flowers and cypress leaves for All Saints' Day (also called All Hallows' Day). In some other cultures, a "day of the dead" is celebrated on October 31, which is All Hallows' Eve—Halloween.

El día de los muertos is celebrated throughout Central America and Mexico. But the huge tissue-paper kites are flown only by the people of Santiago de Sacatepéquez.

GUATEMALA

GUATEMALA

EL BAILE DE LA CONQUISTA

(THE DANCE OF THE CONQUISTADORS)

At special times during the year the main plaza of the market town of Chichicastenango, in Guatemala's western highlands, is taken over by *El baile de la conquista*, the Dance of the Conquistadors. Elaborately costumed and masked characters perform a choreographed historical pageant commemorating the Spanish conquest of the Maya in the sixteenth century.

Guatemala is the only Central American country with a large Indian population. Forty-four percent of all Guatemalans are Mayan Indians, and they are proud of their heritage. Many Indian women dress as they have for centuries—in colorful handwoven clothing—not just on holidays, but every day. And nowhere is this pride more in evidence than in Chichicastenango, a center of Mayan culture.

El baile de la conquista **is enacted throughout Guatemala to celebrate special occasions.**

(ABOVE) The Moors of North Africa conquered Spain in the eighth century, and their descendants were among the Spanish soldiers who later conquered Guatemala. Some *baile de la conquista* masks are black-faced to represent the Moorish conquistadors. (RIGHT) Some dancers wear plumed and beaded Mayan headdresses that represent conquistador helmets; others wear multicolored sombreros. The wide-brimmed sombrero's name comes from the Spanish word for "shade," *sombra*.

GUATEMALA

BELIZE

CARNIVAL

Carnival, which occurs every February or March, celebrates the Christian holiday of Shrove Tuesday, better known as Mardi Gras, or Fat Tuesday. This is the last day before Lent, the forty days between Ash Wednesday and Easter Sunday, when Catholics traditionally give up favorite foods and pastimes. In many countries around the world, carnival is a totally uninhibited party before the long Lenten fast begins. Anything goes during carnival!

In San Pedro—a small town on Ambergris Caye, which is the largest of the Belizean barrier islands—carnival lasts for three days. Strolling costumed players fill the dusty, sun-baked streets with music and dancing. Wherever an audience gathers, they stop to perform minimusicals called *comparsas,* especially in front of shops, where the shopkeepers pay them to entertain. Then on Mardi Gras night, prizes are awarded for the best *comparsas.*

In the past, *comparsa* performers would paint their faces and arms as part of their costumes. Then other people started painting themselves, just for fun. Today it's the children who coat one another (and anyone else they can find) with a mixture of paint, flour, and raw egg. During carnival the streets of San Pedro overflow with merry people splashed with color from head to toe.

(ABOVE) **A troupe of young folk dancers step lively for a gathering crowd. Performers of all ages compete for the** *comparsa* **prize. (LEFT) These children have just spotted someone to splatter with their pop bottles full of pastel paints.**

SEMANA SANTA

(HOLY WEEK)

The week before Easter is celebrated with great fervor throughout the tiny country of El Salvador, where it is known as *semana santa*, or Holy Week. This Christian holiday, which occurs every March or April, commemorates the last days in the life of Jesus, his death by crucifixion on Good Friday, and his resurrection on Easter Sunday. Throughout Central America, Good Friday is the holiest day of all.

The town of Sonsonate in western El Salvador was founded in 1552 by conquistadors, who brought with them the Catholic religion, as well as Spanish customs that are still practiced today. One custom is to decorate the streets with *alfombras* for the Good Friday procession. All day Thursday, people of all ages kneel in the streets to create these "carpets," using sawdust, pine needles, flowers, and powdered dyes. The brightly colored *alfombras* depict everything from Mayan Indian symbols to favorite cartoon characters—whatever inspires the artists.

On Good Friday, costumed townspeople reverently re-create the journey of Jesus to his execution. Priests, people in biblical costumes, and teams carrying statues of Jesus and the town's patron saints slowly make their way through streets jammed with spectators. After the procession and crowds have passed, nothing is left of the *alfombras* but trampled petals and swirls of colors in the dust.

(ABOVE) One family has created a cheerful cartoon penguin *alfombra* to brighten the route for the Good Friday procession. (RIGHT) This young artist's *alfombra* urges spectators to let Jesus into their hearts.

EL SALVADOR

EL SALVADOR

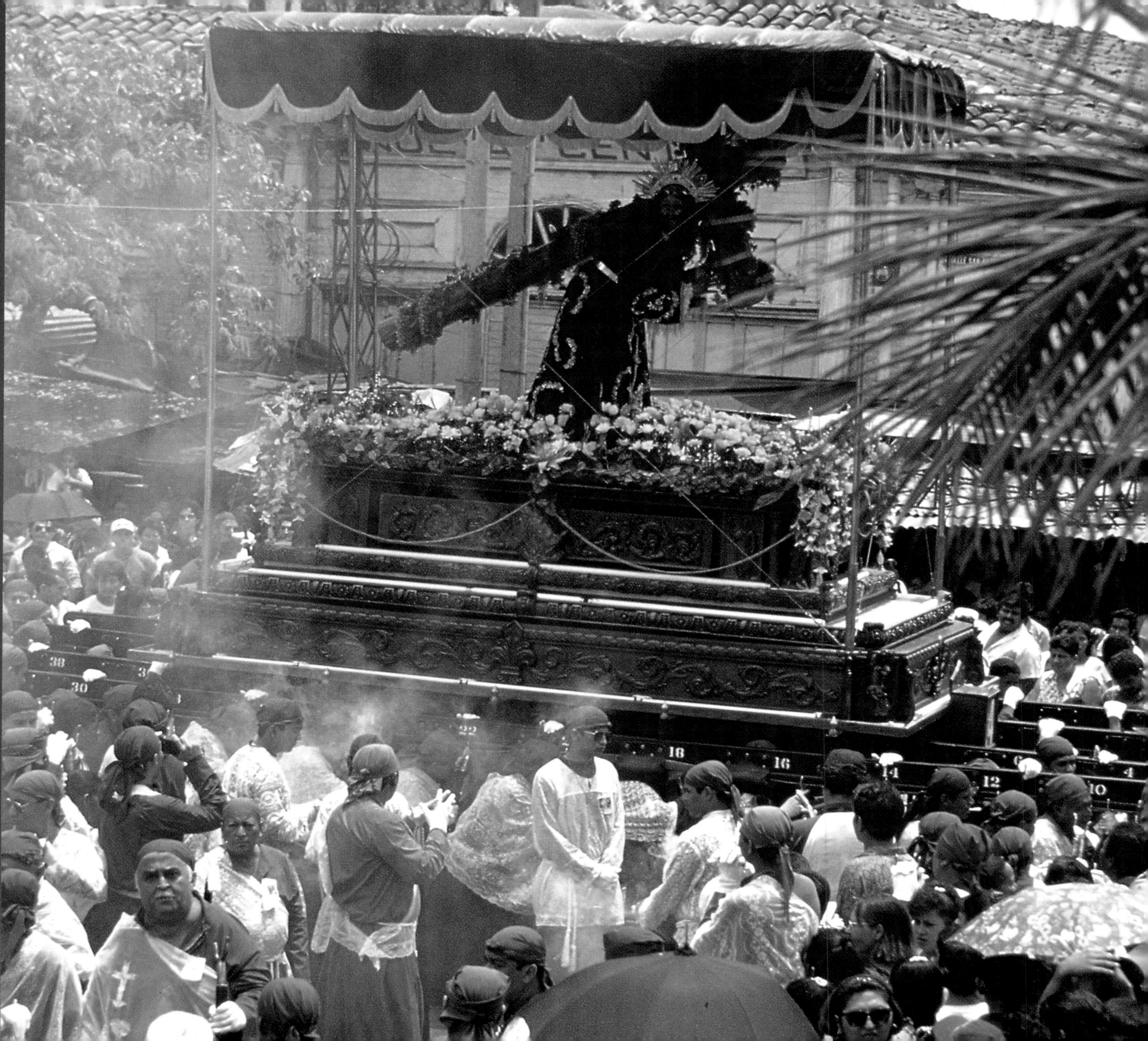

Hundreds of townspeople donate their time and talents to present the Good Friday passion play: a reenactment of the events leading up to Jesus' crucifixion. (THIS PAGE) In the village square, costumed "Romans" dramatize Jesus' trial before Pontius Pilate. (FACING PAGE) Teams of strong men (wearing the purple kerchiefs) take turns carrying a heavy statue of Jesus through the streets of Sonsonate.

SAN JOSÉ FAIR

Every year from March 15 to 20, the Honduran village of Copán Ruinas, located near the Guatemalan border, holds a fair in honor of its patron saint, San José (Saint Joseph).

Copán Ruinas is named for the spectacular ruins of the Mayan city of Copán, less than a mile away. The villagers take pride in both their Spanish and Mayan heritages, and the San José fair mixes elements borrowed from both cultures. For five days, food and craft booths pack Copán Ruinas's main plaza. Colorful piñatas, filled with treats, dangle above eager children waiting impatiently for their turn to attack. In the cool of the evening, folk dancers and musicians entertain the crowds.

On the morning of March 19—the Catholic feast day of San José—the entire village gathers to honor its patron saint. Everyone attends a special outdoor mass. Then as a band plays briskly, the statue of San José, dressed in a straw hat and black cape, is carried through mobbed streets. That night, the people of Copán Ruinas wind up the celebration with theatrical performances based on ancient Mayan rituals.

(ABOVE) Copán was a great Mayan city-state that flourished for close to two thousand years. Around 900 A.D. it mysteriously collapsed, leaving massive monuments to be taken over by the jungle. (RIGHT) Whack! A little girl swings with all her might to break the piñata and release its sweet shower of candy.

HONDURAS

HONDURAS

The preservation of both ancient Mayan and Spanish cultures through performance is an important part of the San José fair.

VIRGIN OF MASAYA CELEBRATION

The town of Masaya rests in the shadow of the great double-crested Volcán Masaya. On March 16, 1772, the volcano erupted, threatening to destroy the town. In an act of great courage and faith, the local priest removed a statue of the Virgin Mary from the church and frantically carried her up and down the streets of Masaya. As local people tell the story, the sky suddenly became dark and cloudy and it started to rain, putting an end to the volcanic fires about to engulf the town. It was considered a great miracle, and every year on March 16 the miracle is remembered and celebrated.

First thing in the morning, a group of local women arrives at the church to dress the Virgin and adorn her with flowers. After the statue is robed, the townspeople stream by, touching a hand or foot to receive her blessing. Then the Virgin of Masaya is veiled, placed atop a platform covered by a canopy, and carried up and down the cobbled streets, much as she was in 1772. The whole town joins the parade, marching to the music of a simple brass band.

Despite the natural disasters and bloody warfare that have frequently plagued Nicaragua, the Virgin of Masaya celebration has been held every year since 1772.

(ABOVE) The village of Masaya rests beside a crater lake beneath the great double-crested Volcán Masaya. One of the craters is still active and constantly spews smoke and steam. (LEFT) There is a small burn mark on the delicate hand of the statue, and everyone in Masaya says it was caused by the 1772 volcanic eruption.

COLUMBUS DAY

Columbus Day is celebrated every October 12 throughout the Americas. On this day in 1492, the Italian explorer Christopher Columbus, sailing for Spain's Queen Isabella and King Ferdinand, landed in the Bahamas and "discovered" the Americas for Europe. In many Latin American countries, including Costa Rica, the holiday is also called *El día de la raza,* or "the Day of the Race," for the new race of people, called *mestizo,* created from the intermarriage of arriving Europeans with native peoples.

Thousands of visitors pour into Puerto Limón (also called Limón) for Columbus Day, which often turns into several days of raucous parades and music, singing, and dancing in the streets. The holiday is celebrated with particular enthusiasm in Limón because Columbus landed less than a mile from here on September 18, 1502, during his fourth and final voyage to the Americas. He stayed for seventeen days, noticed that some of the natives wore magnificent gold ornaments, and named the place Costa Rica, meaning "rich coast."

Many people of African ancestry have made their homes along the Caribbean coast of Central America. In Puerto Limón, Costa Ricans of African ancestry celebrate their contribution to the country's rich mix of cultures during the Columbus Day festivities.

PANAMA

CARNIVAL

Carnival is a major holiday in many countries in Europe and the Americas, but each nation brings its own special style to the Mardi Gras celebration. In Panama, the old colonial town of Las Tablas was settled by conquistadors in the sixteenth century, and its people preserve many Spanish traditions to this day. Panama's national costume for women, the elegant *pollera*, is of Spanish origin. Most of these intricately embroidered ruffled dresses are made just outside Las Tablas and are to be seen in all their glory there.

Pollera-clad women of all ages are everywhere you look during carnival: in beauty pageants, on parade floats, and dancing in the streets among the throngs who flock to Las Tablas for four days and nights of nonstop partying. Panama is close to the equator, so even though carnival is celebrated in February or March, it's so hot during the day that everyone looks forward to the water fights that break out everywhere.

No matter whether it's satin and sequins or a lacy *pollera*, carnival is a time to dress up in fancy costumes.

(ABOVE) During carnival the party never seems to stop. Night or day, wherever there's a band playing, crowds of people gather. (RIGHT) In the heat of the day, water sprayed from a fire hose offers cooling relief. The crowd screams with glee while being soaked to the bone.

PANAMA

A young dancer works on her moves for a *comparsa* she'll perform for carnival in the town of San Pedro on Ambergris Caye (pronounced *key*), an island off the coast of Belize.

The text type is 14-point Meridien.
Text copyright © 1997 by Joe Viesti and Diane Hall
Illustrations copyright © 1997 by Joe Viesti
Published by Lothrop, Lee & Shepard Books, an imprint of Morrow Junior Books
a division of William Morrow and Company, Inc., 1350 Avenue of the Americas, New York, NY 10019

Printed in Singapore at Tien Wah Press.

1 2 3 4 5 6 7 8 9 10

Library of Congress Cataloging-in-Publication Data
Viesti, Joseph F.
Celebrate! in Central America/by Joe Viesti and Diane Hall; photographed by Joe Viesti.
p. cm.
Summary: Describes the background and customs associated with some of the festivals of Central America.
ISBN 0-688-15161-2 (trade)—ISBN 0-688-15162-0 (library)
1. Festivals—Central America—Juvenile literature.   2. Central America—Social life and customs—Juvenile literature.
[1. Festivals—Central America.   2. Central America—Social life and customs.]
I. Hall, Diane.   II. Title.   GT3933.V54 1997   394.269728—dc21   96-6716   CIP AC